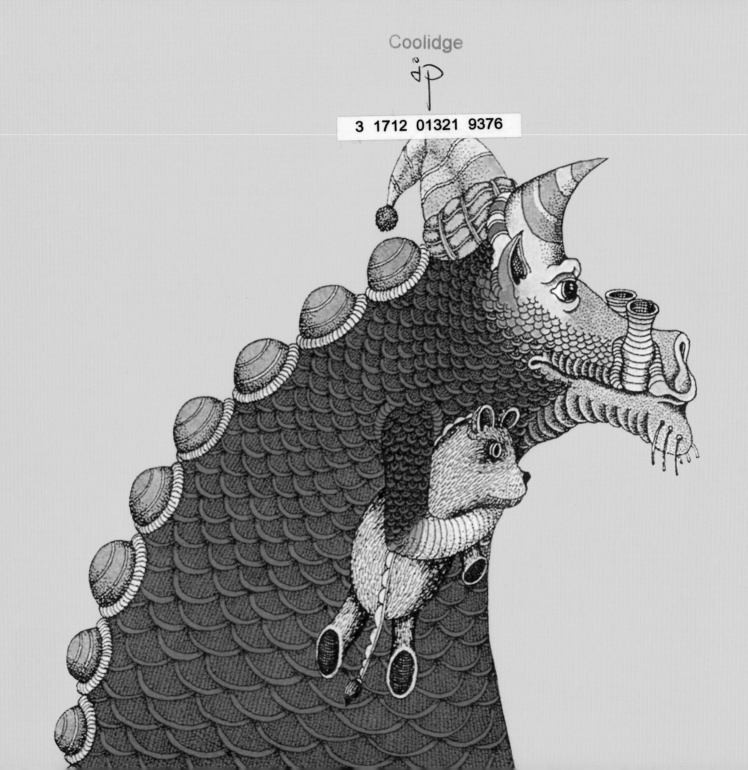

ONE DRAGON'S DREAM

PETER PAVEY

CANDLEWICK PRESS

One dragon had a dream

2 that two turkeys teased him,

3 three tigers told him off,

4 and four frogs seized him.

5 Five cranky kangaroos
hopped around and fenced him in.

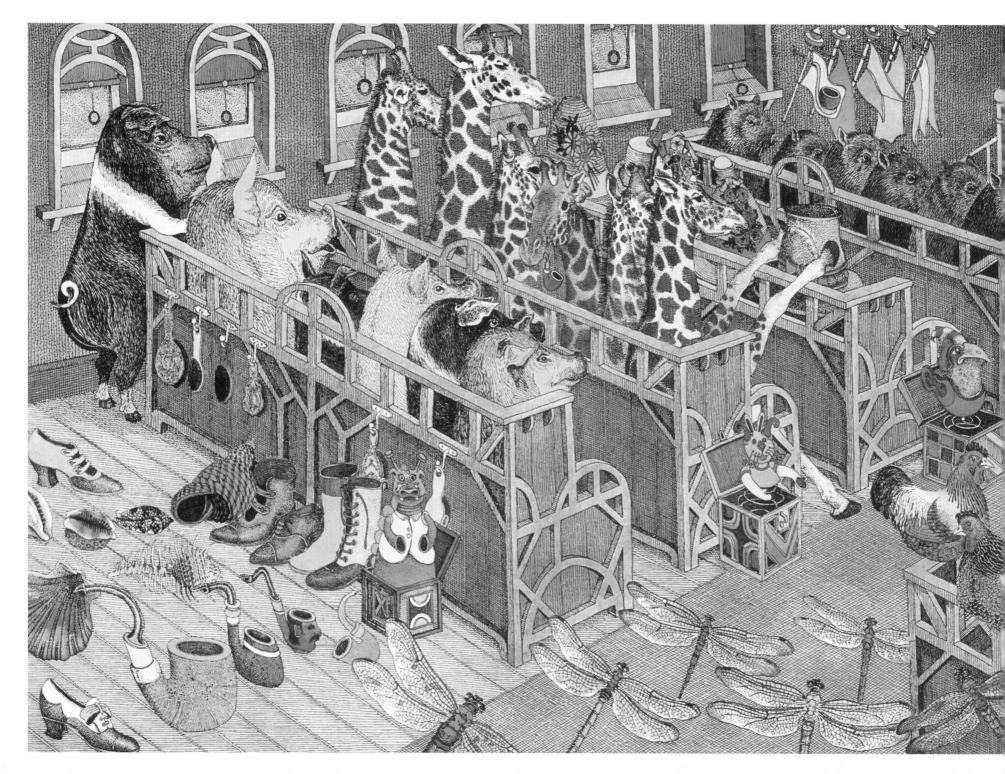

6 Six stern storks tried him and sentenced him.

7 Seven slippery sea lions—
off to jail they juggled him.

Eight great elephants—
in balloons they smuggled him.

9 Nine nimble numbats
sewed him up with thread.

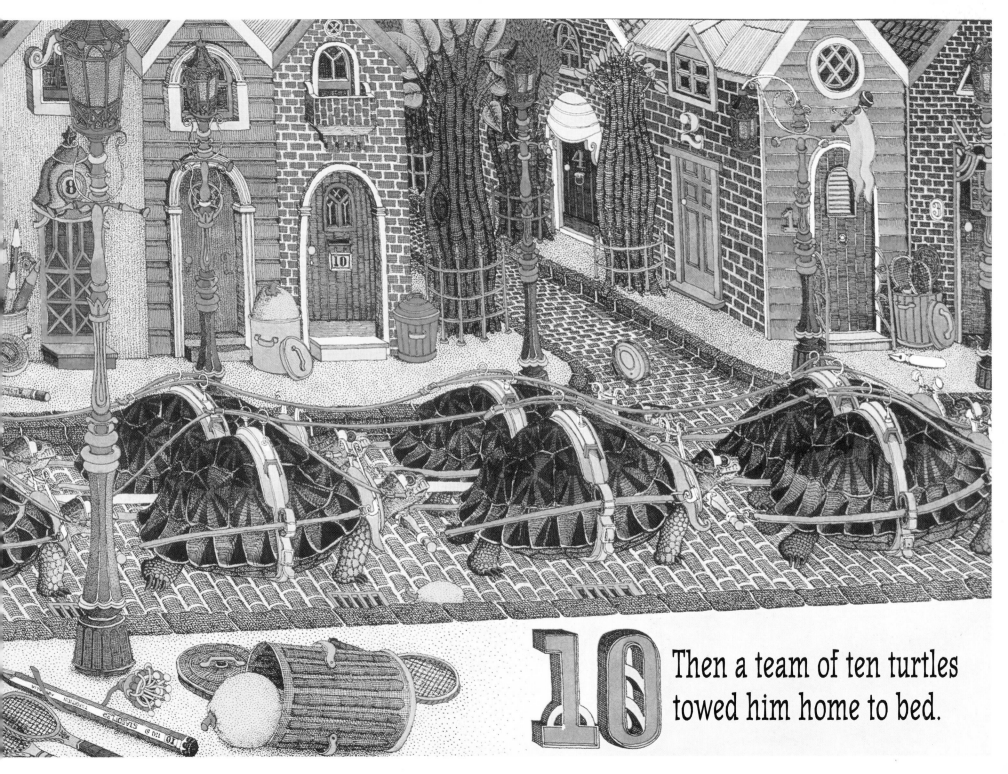

Then a team of ten turtles
towed him home to bed.

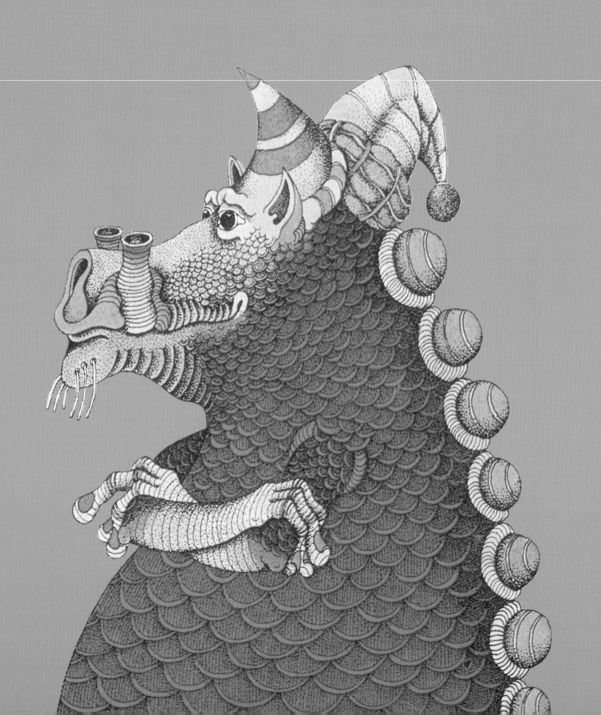

For Ron, Jay, Miche, and Rosie

First Candlewick Press edition 2009

Library of Congress Cataloging-in-Publication Data
Pavey, Peter.
One dragon's dream / by Peter Pavey. — 1st ed.
p. cm.
Summary: As a dragon dreams of turkeys, tigers, kangaroos, and seals,
the reader can count the items hidden within the dream.
ISBN 978-0-7636-4470-3
[1. Stories in rhyme. 2. Dreams — Fiction. 3. Dragons — Fiction. 4. Counting.]
I. Title.
PZ8.3.P2737On 2009
[E] — dc22 2009007511

2 4 6 8 10 9 7 5 3 1

Printed in China

This book was typeset in Journal.
The illustrations were done in ink and watercolor.

Candlewick Press
99 Dover Street
Somerville, Massachusetts 02144

visit us at www.candlewick.com